# A Journey Within

LouAnne Ludwig

BALBOA.
PRESS
A DIVISION OF HAY HOUSE

Balboa Press books may be ordered through booksellers or by contacting:

Balboa Press
A Division of Hay House
1663 Liberty Drive
Bloomington, IN 47403
www.balboapress.com
1 (877) 407-4847

Because of the dynamic nature of the Internet, any web addresses or links contained in this book may have changed since publication and may no longer be valid. The views expressed in this work are solely those of the author and do not necessarily reflect the views of the publisher, and the publisher hereby disclaims any responsibility for them.

The author of this book does not dispense medical advice or prescribe the use of any technique as a form of treatment for physical, emotional, or medical problems without the advice of a physician, either directly or indirectly. The intent of the author is only to offer information of a general nature to help you in your quest for emotional and spiritual well-being. In the event you use any of the information in this book for yourself, which is your constitutional right, the author and the publisher assume no responsibility for your actions.

Any people depicted in stock imagery provided by Getty Images are models, and such images are being used for illustrative purposes only. Certain stock imagery © Getty Images.

Print information available on the last page.

ISBN: 978-1-9822-0224-8 (sc)
ISBN: 978-1-9822-0223-1 (hc)
ISBN: 978-1-9822-0225-5 (e)

Library of Congress Control Number: 2018904424

Balboa Press rev. date: 04/20/2018

# CONTENTS

# ACKNOWLEDGMENTS

*A* special thanks to my husband, Steve, who was at the forefront of my lunacy as I went through many changes while experimenting with the tools I present here. I especially appreciate that he did not decide I had gone off the deep end when I asked him to honor my request not to utilize poison while dealing with an incessant barrage of an ant infestation much like the invasions experienced by our main character, Alexander. He did not know what I went through behind the scenes or he would certainly have questioned my sanity. As it stands, however, he appreciates the peaceful and pleasant landscape of our household now that I have firmly established the habits proposed here.

I give my deepest thanks also to my daughter, Jenifer Woods, who brainstormed with me for hours on end as we utilized and worked with the intricacies of these beautiful exercises.

My friends Ben and Zora Skinner and Susan Ray, I am forever grateful for the time you spent helping me stay in the bounds of my rational mind as I took my journey within.

# Introduction

Here is a story about a boy who is not really a boy but a woman who has been through all this and more. She dragged herself through the trenches to learn what she needed to learn in an experiential manner to write this book.

There were times when I was ready to admit defeat and go back to living as an overworked, stressed-out real estate agent. But instead I persevered.

Most people find their opportunities for spiritual growth either through their church or by seeing life through the eyes of science. I have experienced a mixture of the two, gathering my insights from both perspectives. I started in one place, moved to the other, then back again, finally segueing to a mixture of both. I now see all-encompassing love in the form of Pure Positive Energy. This was achieved by my finding a personal connection to the Divine that I could identify with in an affectionate manner.

This spiritual energy was personified for a time in my path so I could come to know the very special feeling of love emanating from it and carry this forward into my current belief system. The love that pours forth from Pure Source Energy easily paves the way for us to find the grace we seek in our lives. Wisdom and knowing are always shown to us in ways we can comfortably absorb, though there are times when we decide by our own actions to take a longer, more arduous journey. Always, the concept of freedom of choice is paramount in our experience here on earth. We can decide to tune in to Source Energy before making our decisions, go it on our own, or land somewhere in between.

The pages of this book hold a wealth of concepts that I have studied diligently from various sources over the years but never mastered until I finally decided to put all my emphasis of thought on how to change my way of looking at everyone and everything. The resulting path brought me to the writing you see here, which I researched in the most personal of ways.

Many times, the antics that played themselves out before me would be unbelievable to anyone else who would look at my experiences and wonder what was going on. No one could know it was merely my way of living the tools I would present in exaggerated forms that created these scenarios for me. There was no other way I could have witnessed such outlandish events except by my attracting them with my intention to learn these things completely and at breakneck speed.

At times, a lesson would manifest in a ridiculous manner just to find out if I would laugh or be disheartened, thereby giving me further feedback on how well I was doing with the learning I had set forth for myself.

In the beginning, I was often frustrated and sometimes even distraught that I could not bring myself to the level of excellence I expected of myself as I worked—unbeknownst to me—on my perfectionism for example. I would bring forth unusual situations to work on just to see if I would realize it was just another of my traps set to pull me into its grasp.

As time went on, however, I got into the flow of this daily barrage of crazy-ass occurrences that would appear before me. I even came to expect wild antics that would catapult me forward just as our main character, Alexander, was catapulted in his journey in this book.

The main purpose of this book is to lend credence to the mind-training techniques many of us read about and sometimes even do workbook exercises on expecting we will come away from a book more enlightened and better equipped to flourish.

I'll often pick up a marvelous book and become so entrenched in the subject that I think it will never leave me. Inevitably after finishing the book though, life would expand and pull me back into its drama before I could use the tools I had just learned.

This book is designed to circumvent that reoccurring pattern by being read completely through the first time. This will allow you to take note of Alexander's progression in how he perceives the godlike figure and other such subtleties as each chapter or story builds on the last.

When you have an opportunity to utilize a method taught in any chapter, reread just that story, which in itself is a delight and can stand alone for that reason. This rereading will reinforce the lesson for you, and you will find yourself well on your way to mastering each of the highly valuable tools presented here.

Before long, every tool in the book will become a process that you can automatically utilize every day. Keep this book in easy reach; you will find enchantment every time you refresh yourself by rereading a chapter. Every time you immerse yourself in the story line, you will see additional nuances of wisdom that did not appear to you before.

My highest intention is that you will enjoy reading this simple yet complex story that lays out a version of the meaning of life while offering immense lessons that will enhance your life in astounding ways as you use the ideas presented here by these characters and their journeys within.

# CHAPTER 1

## *The Beginning of Time*

O nce upon a time, a young boy was living a normal life in the scheme of things. One morning he awoke and found himself transplanted from his most comfortable of beds to a remote, secluded island in the middle of the ocean.

Of course, he knew he was only dreaming, for what he saw was way off the scale of anything he could ever have imagined possibly happening to a boy who spent his days going to school, riding his bike, and playing with other kids in his normal, little neighborhood.

At first, it was fun going along with the dream. He enjoyed running between the sand dunes, diving into the waves as they crashed on the shore, chasing seagulls, and breathing the crisp, fresh air without a care in the world.

But as the day wore on and his stomach began to growl, he slowly realized there might be more to his dream than he had suspected. For one thing, it seemed a bit too realistic. He began to wonder exactly how long a dream like this could actually last. Things were just not adding up.

The reality of his hunger forced him to conclude that he had to act as though his dream might go on forever. So without another thought, he began to forage for food. His escapades that day had taken him far and wide, and he had seen no sign of others. When he came upon a small cave tucked in a hillside near the beach, he decided to call this his new home. Thankfully, he discovered many coconut and banana trees in the vicinity. That fueled his budding thoughts that something greater than he was watching over him.

As nightfall crept closer, he wished he could start a fire, but by then, he was quite exhausted. He lay on the bed of grass he had prepared and pulled his trusty blanket tightly around himself. He was so relieved that the blanket and a few other necessities had made their way to the island with him. Snuggling in for a good night's sleep, he felt as though all the voices of the jungle were coming eerily to life and feeding his already overactive imagination. Just as he thought he would never be able to put aside his growing fears and apprehension, exhaustion won out and sleep overtook him.

The next morning, our unlikely young beachcomber awoke to find himself nose to nose with a curious monkey who had wandered into the cave and was exploring the curves of the boy's face with his arched finger. As the shock of this rude encounter began to wear off, the boy sat there dumbfounded; he realized there was no way this was only a dream. That realization almost crushed him. Scenario after scenario of scary and potentially dangerous situations ran across the screen of his vivid imagination. *I can't possibly survive here by myself!* he thought. *This can't be happening. I want to go home!*

But happening it was. Before long, he whipped himself into such a dither that helplessness overtook the young boy who just the day before had slain dragons through the sand dunes and set up shelter while piling in a food supply. He was cowering under his blanket and crying and shaking for hours on end. It was as though his entire world had come crashing down on him. As far as he was concerned, it had. Eventually, sleep overpowered him, and he drifted off once again into its welcome embrace.

When he awoke to the break of a new day, he decided it made no sense to allow himself the luxury of pouting any longer. By then, his hunger was uppermost in his mind. He dove eagerly into the stack of bananas and coconuts he had gathered upon his arrival. After a few false starts, he became somewhat adept at carefully breaking coconuts so he could suck the water from them before peeling the meat out for his hungry consumption. He knew he would need other foods to supplement his stash, but for the time being, he was happy to sit surrounded by broken coconut shells and banana peels.

Before long, the monkey from the day prior returned armed with new antics to keep the young boy from contemplating his shocking new situation. He would swing from vines and swoop down just close enough to playfully swat the boy on the head. The gaiety was infectious.

With a full stomach and the temptation of fun brought by his newfound friend, the boy launched in to a rollicking game of chase; he filled the air with peals of laughter. He and the monkey were so wrapped up in their delightful play that at first, neither noticed the deep silence that had come upon the place. When they finally sensed the enormous change in the air, they stopped and looked up to see a glowing figure with flowing robes and a large walking stick standing nearby.

At first, the boy was taken aback. Fear rose in him. But as he took in the scene, he began to feel a warm sense of serenity wash over him. Still too scared to say a word, he waited to see what might happen next. As the mysterious figure moved toward him, the glow slowly changed into the image of a wise and all-knowing man.

That was the beginning of a new and exciting life for the boy. He had found his amazing mentor who would lead him to new heights of knowledge and appreciation in the confines of his sleeping mind and carry him to a place of knowing. From there, he would eventually return to his family home and bring with him new riches of thought for all to share.

# CHAPTER 2

# A Meeting of Epic Proportions

O nce upon a time, a bright child named Alexander found himself inexplicably stranded on a remote, secluded, tropical island in the middle of the Pacific Ocean. He was completely alone with the exception of his pet monkey, Manuka, and a mysterious stranger who had appeared out of nowhere one day and then disappeared without a trace minutes later. Alexander saw this mystical stranger from time to time in the distance and always framed with a most beautiful orb of light. But as soon as eye contact was made, he would again fade from view.

One day, the boy set out with his monkey to see if they could get a closer look at the source of the elusive light. No sooner had they left the confines of the boy's cave than the glowing figure appeared before them. No words were spoken, but the boy somehow knew clearly that the wise one intended to impart something of great importance to him. His head filled with glorious pictures of a life brimming with lovely visions of spectacular natural phenomena. His family back home was flourishing and joyful; his home life there was almost a utopia. The ways of all were uplifting as they took remarkable joy in each other.

Gone was the petty bickering that used to hide around every corner. In its place were pleasant and supportive conversations and comments along with gaiety and laughter. Even their home had changed in subtle yet profound ways. Furniture had been rearranged in a more open and welcoming way, and some of it had been replaced with artifacts of glorious times gone by, bringing on a feeling of timeless beauty and abundance.

So remarkable was Alexander's vision that his entire body felt a vibrational resonance. He felt as though his insides were about to explode through the protective covering of his skin. He felt larger than life even in his tiny body.

When at last he opened his eyes, he saw a matrix-like screen of falling electrical lines partially obscuring the view of the area surrounding the opening of his cave home. It was as though he had visited yet another level of reality and was halfway between both.

The curious boy discovered a new aspect of himself as he wandered in the jungle attempting to shake off the incredible experience he had just had. He peered into a pond of water, and on his face, he saw a pair of enormous, dark eyes peering back at him. His pupils were wide open, and he could see completely down to his soul and beyond. He turned to ask the master what that was all about, but the wise one had faded from view. Realizing he was alone again, Alexander snapped back into his prior self-experience leaving the magic of those moments in his memory.

# Chapter 3

## *Intention Setting*

Once upon a time, a boy named Alexander was living all alone on a remote, deserted, tropical island. He was accompanied solely by his pet monkey, Manuka, and a wise old sage who inhabited a mountaintop far away and allowed himself to be seen only when it suited him.

One day, Alexander and Manuka were playing on the beach when they heard a loud explosion. They ran into the jungle toward the sound. In a clearing, they saw the glowing orb of light in the distance that told them they would soon lay eyes on the mysterious man of the mountaintop.

Manuka ran off leaving Alexander alone to face the wise man again. It seemed he was always alone when they were together, but he had no time to further contemplate that anomaly; the old man was aptly making his way to the clearing where the young boy stood trembling.

Though he remembered the easy feeling of complete love that emanated from this man who came from the light, he had been moved so profoundly in the past by these encounters that he still didn't know what to expect. The power radiating from this wise one was so intense and unfamiliar that he couldn't help feeling frightened.

Here was an opportunity to speak directly to this elder, who was clearly concentrating on giving more insights to the quaking boy, but when Alexander opened his mouth to speak, he could not utter a sound. It was as though the sage controlled all that surrounded them with the raising of his hand. The symphony of birdsong floating by just a moment before ceased as a hush came over the meadow. Then, just as suddenly as the silence had appeared, it vanished, and the air was once again filled with melodic enchantment.

The sage planted the knowledge of heaven's prayer descending on earth in those moments that found all nature in hushed anticipation. The prayer was this.

> It is the intent of our heavenly Father that we pray faithfully with the receiving of each meal and upon rising in the morning and retiring at night.

> It is the intent of us all that we welcome His blessings unto us all in these times and be grateful for all that is done for us in His holy name, amen.

This completely confused the boy, who had been raised to know God only as a distant component of the world who was too busy to really keep up with the details other than creation in the beginning of time. Alexander suddenly found his voice again and began to ask question after question.

"Who are you? Where did you come from? How did I get here? Where are my parents? Do they know I'm gone? If so, do they miss me? Do they want me back?"

He would have eagerly kept at it, but the hand of the sage rose again, that time silencing only the boy.

"I Am that I Am," said the man of the light. "You know me as God Almighty, but you don't know me at all, and I am here to change that and bring about some major changes in and around you."

The boy stared in confounded silence.

"I will give you lessons that will carry you to extreme heights if you allow yourself to listen and assimilate what I will tell you and demonstrate to you, my dear boy. I am here in this form to allow everyone on the earth to come into special knowing of my abilities to give all humanity the tools necessary to live their lives in harmony with each other and to enjoy the exquisite bounty available for all to share.

"These tools have been at your disposal since the beginning of time, but only a rare few of you have mastered them to the degree that would bring about the changes necessary to give mankind the hope it needs to turn things around, my son. Jesus Christ was one such man, and Buddha was another. They were magnificently effective in their times, but the world is in such a critical placement right now that I decided I must take significant action. So here you are.

"This is the answer to all your questions, for your parents are oblivious to your presence here and will wonder what became of you when you return only because of the miraculous changes you will have undergone in such a short time. From their limited perspective that is. You on the other hand will feel at times that you are spending years here on my private island while at other times you will think time is speeding gleefully by.

"One of the ways you will find the time to pass more quickly will be by paving the way of your daily activities. This easy process will bring you untold benefits. Each time you are heading into a situation in which you anticipate trouble or even when you want to make a fun time all the more pleasing, you will give thought to what you will see as your highest expectation in those moments. I see this as another opportunity to pray to God Almighty, but others might just phrase it like so:

'My intention here is to enjoy my day with Manuka and easily find plenty of food and clean, healthy water while I'm at it.'

A prayerful version of this might be something like this:

'Heavenly Father, I pray I will enjoy my day with Manuka and easily find plenty of food and clean, healthy water while I'm at it.'

"You will be amazed at the changes this little tool will bring your way, my dear Alexander. This focusing of your intentions in a present, positive manner is key to manifesting exactly what you want to experience.

"This is only the beginning of the magic-like gifts I have to offer you as you study with me here. Please take these words with you to your cave and contemplate them thoroughly. At the end of the day, I expect you will have used both of these tools several times and are feeling at home with them. You will soon see the amazing fruit of your labor."

The great sage once again faded into the landscape and out of sight of the poor boy, who was standing there dumbfounded at all he had just heard. His work was most assuredly cut out for him, so he headed to his cave, where Manuka was eagerly awaiting him.

# CHAPTER 4

# Mindfulness and Becoming Aware of the Voices in Your Head

O nce upon a time, a boy named Alexander was living on an island in the middle of the ocean. He was joined by a special mentor who had become quite close to him there. This mentor was a peculiar sort in that he appeared and disappeared at will, and the boy never knew when these visits might occur.

One morning, Alexander was playing with his favorite companion, a monkey by the name of Manuka. The two frolicked so joyously that at times, the boy wished he would never have to leave this wondrous place.

There were other times, however, that he was upset at the thought of never returning home to his beloved family. They meant the world to him, and he feared they might forget ever having had such a boy as himself if much more time passed. Each time he let that thought come into his head and dance around a bit, it would turn into all sorts of frightful what-ifs, and soon, he would be so upset that he would become quite grumpy and no fun whatsoever to the irrepressible Manuka.

In the middle of this grump session, the one who called Himself God again appeared out of nowhere causing Alexander to startle at the timing of His Holiness's abrupt arrival.

"I am here to set aside some comfort-seeking tools for you, my little one. I know you are lonely and afraid, and my ardent wish is to ease your burden and give you pathways to great joy. You will be relieved to discover that this lesson will bring you the peace you are seeking, my son, and you will never again find yourself upset if you will only follow these simple directions.

"When you realize your imagination is getting away from you, notice that it is as though little voices of yours are spouting off in your mind. As soon as you recognize that voices are commenting on whatever is passing through your mind, you will realize those voices are not there to serve you but to strangle you with fears and suppositions.

"Even the voices of good reason are there to strangle you at times when they are coming at you hard to confuse your accurate reasoning skills. When they rattle on and on without your having a hand in it so to speak, they will only tangle you up and make you question the serious discernment you may have already completed on the subject.

"Even the times you have not settled on a decision about something, you would be better served by silencing the voices and allowing your mind reason to take over. You can do this easily by relaxing into the recesses of your mind and observing the voices until they stop. They will do so almost immediately when they realize they are being watched by the real you, the observer of your thoughts.

"If you apply this lesson to your everyday life such as when you are letting your imagination get the best of you about your family situation or worrying about finding enough food to sustain you, you will become master of your destiny. Your thoughts carry the weight of the world in these situations, and that is just too much weight for any man—or boy—to carry."

Alexander was perplexed by these instructions and made this clear to his beloved mentor. But the resulting reply was the usual: "Take it back with you and give it some good thought. But don't let those voices take over the conversation, for then, we'll be right back where we started!"

Just as the boy turned to head back to his cave, the wise man added, "If you can become successful with this tool, you will easily master the next—stay mindful, which is keeping your mind completely focused on the present-moment happenings including thoughts, emotions, and experiences without judging them.

"This little gem will bring you to places of inner peace you've never imagined. It will allow the universe to unleash its forces and balance and harmonize all around you in amazing ways. At first, you will find yourself fading from this practice with each distraction but then returning because you have set your intention on remaining mindful at all times. This practice is such an ebb and flow as you work through it, but mastery of it is attainable as long as you maintain your efforts on its behalf.

"The grand prize here is that your experience of life will change dramatically. For now, the universal forces can convene on your behalf, and you will not be getting in the way so much anymore. You do not have to master these techniques perfectly. Each that becomes natural to you will feed the forces of a powerful life directed by your decisions in each moment to make your thoughts create the most amazing life you could imagine for yourself and for those who surround you and are benefitting by your thoughts even without their knowing it. Tomorrow I will tell you exactly how this sharing of thoughts can become your favorite tool. And for now, I must bid you adieu."

# CHAPTER 5

# Giving Thanks and Listing Positive Attributes

O nce upon a time, a boy named Alexander found himself mysteriously placed on an island in the South Pacific. He had no one to talk to except his trusty monkey companion, Manuka, and a very strange and glorious being who resided high up a mountain. This being had professed Himself to be God Almighty to the boy, but it didn't matter to Alexander who the man was;

it mattered only that this unusual one who appeared and disappeared on a whim treated the boy with utmost respect and loving care.

One day, the boy was busily gathering coconuts and other such delectables to adorn his table at meal time when out of nowhere the man called God appeared and asked Alexander to stop what he was doing and sit by His side. He wanted to see if the boy would follow that simple command though his arms were full of his culinary treasures.

The boy immediately set down his bounty and bounded over to see what gems of wisdom his master had for him that day. In the past, though the lessons were difficult at first, the child's diligent efforts to assimilate them in his everyday activities had paid off handsomely.

He had learned to be grateful to God in the form of prayer for his meals, and he found that this seemed to multiply his food supply. His morning prayers of gratefulness served to bring him to a better place in his mind to begin his wondrous days and set himself up for a delightful day. His evening prayers of thanks were a calming reassurance that all was well though he was in this faraway land without a snip of connection with his loving family, whom he missed dearly. Instead of sleeping fitfully and worrying, he slept restfully and woke the next morning refreshed and rejuvenated.

The paving technique was astounding in its value. It helped him focus on his intentions—what he wanted to do and accomplish—and it often smoothed the way to a most beautiful outcome like magic.

Becoming aware of the voices in his head was a real eye-opener; it made him realize that whenever he followed his master's advice on the subject, he could keep himself from spinning out of control and becoming overly upset about almost anything. Every now and then, he found he just could not shake the voices, so he would make a mental note to ask God for further help with such more difficult times.

Mindfulness was the latest thing his master had taught him, and he loved the effects of this enchanting, peace-bringing technique. He had not known that merely keeping his thoughts trained on what was happening in the moment could allow the flow of life around him to lift its wings, soar into space, and return with exactly what he needed for the next moment and the next. The concept was so simple and yet so powerful in that it could provide for him if only he willingly focused on the here and now.

Alexander had been so used to his mind taking off into the future and worrying about what might come next or revisiting the past and filling him with self-recrimination about how it could have gone better. He was amazed at how the simplest ways could bring the biggest payoffs.

That morning, Alexander was anxious to hear what nuggets the sage might impart to him. He was already so full of these new ways of thinking that it was hard for him to believe there could be more. Scampering up in front of his master, he found a seat on a rock and settled in for another amazing lesson.

Here, the God one told him how proud he was of the boy's progress. He said that the boy's gratefulness had brought him to such heights in such a short time. That, He said, was the key to most every treasure gleaned from the pack of tools he was already mastering.

He suggested that Alexander take this one step further by concentrating on realizing when he felt the least bit grateful for something that he would thank God or the universe for it. He said this action alone would catapult the boy forward to even more amazing heights and make him realize that everything he wanted would come to pass easily and quickly. The mere action of being thankful for his bounty even in the smallest of increments was a key aspect of their manifestation.

As he was practicing this new tool of thought, his master recommended he also make lists of positive attributes whenever he found himself fussing over something or was agitated. He would usually become upset over someone he was unhappy with, thus causing an uncomfortable situation. If he could just turn his mind then to thinking about what he liked about the person, he would bring his focus back to upliftment, which would bring more positive ideas and thoughts his way. Pretty soon, he would be starting to think better again of the individual, and miraculously, that person's demeanor would turn around almost as if he or she had actually heard what he had said.

That created another way for the boy to easily manifest the joy in life he was always seeking. And so, becoming forever grateful for the master bestowing on him such joyous gifts, he thanked God profusely.

# Chapter 6

# Law of Attraction, Deliberate Creation, and Radical Forgiveness

Once upon a time, a young boy by the name of Alexander lived by himself on an island in the middle of the Pacific. He was not completely alone; he did have a pet monkey, Manuka, and a mentor who lived in a cave on a mountaintop. This one was quite mysterious and called Himself God, but the boy was oblivious to the meaning of that and cared only that he had another person somewhere with him on the island. He also cared that the God man helped him whenever he ran into trouble such as the time the seagulls preyed on his meager stock of food.

This came to pass one day when the boy had been less than careful about how he was storing his left-over food after finishing a meal. He had no idea he should have put away open containers and protect food from the prying eyes and claws of scavengers on the beach. His mother had always been the one to take care of that when they would go to the beach for a picnic back home. On that day, he had a full-fledged army of seagulls fighting him for the little food he had left in the world—from his limited perspective that is.

He had no idea what to do to rid himself of this pesky problem; it seemed the seagulls were everywhere. As soon as he swatted one away, three more would tear away at his precious stockpile of food. They had found their way into his cave, and he found it impossible to get them all to leave at the same time.

Each time he thought he had them eradicated, they would return in full force. That went on it seemed for days. He no longer could take a break even to play with Manuka; he had to spend every waking moment trying to solve this growing problem.

At last, God intervened and told the boy he would need to back off from his attacks on these precious birds; they were doing only what they did when humans forgot to pack up their food. It makes no difference to the gulls that those food containers were coconut shells and banana peels instead of Tupperware or Saran wrap. God said that the youngster would be best served by not thinking about the seagulls whatsoever, that removing them from his consciousness or taking his attention off them would be the answer to all his problems hands down.

The boy set off to do just that. Just as he was busy playing with Manuka again having cleared his mind of this debacle, another seagull appeared out of nowhere and headed straight for the food. Alexander watched in horror until he remembered the instructions he had been given. So he cleared his mind and gleefully went back to playing with his monkey friend. No sooner had he turned his head than another seagull came, and another, and another until the whole cave seemed to be overflowing with them.

This brought the young boy to tears. He ran to his beloved cave, the only semblance of home he knew in those strangest of times. *What can I do? Keeping my mind off these scoundrels is just plain impossible!* He was so incensed at the drama playing out before his eyes that he missed the opportunity to use the tool he had learned. If he would have just remembered to change his thoughts from the rage he was experiencing to making a mental list of positive attributes of these beautiful and interesting birds! Had he done that, the exercise would have been over immediately. But instead he chose the longer route.

For that matter, he could have chosen to place his attention on just about anything in his surroundings, which he loved and appreciated no matter how small or inconsequential. But that's neither here nor there. Instead, the lesson continued.

The boy searched the horizon for his beloved mentor hoping God would show up and bail him out before all that he had worked so hard to stockpile was scattered to kingdom come. No one appeared though, so Alexander was forced to sit on a rock and figure out how to keep his mind from thinking about the biggest problem he could ever imagine.

Before long, the boy was exhausted and depressed. His formerly huge pile of food was down to almost nothing. He had nowhere to turn and no options except to try to kill them; that would surely bring about the end of this tirade.

What he didn't know was that when predators attacked seagulls, the seagulls tended to call out to all their friends and families to lend a hand and fight off the attack. That was exactly what Alexander did not need. He thought he had problems before, but now he had a real army on his hands. Before long, the entire beach was filled with the winged creatures all distressed and screaming.

Poor Alexander was at his wit's end. He could do nothing but surrender to his fate. He knew that as soon as all the food was gone, they would have no further reason to stay, so he waited and watched as they picked him clean.

That was it. He was done. Nothing he could do would change things. Helplessness overtook him as he realized even restocking his food supply would only provide new feasts for the birds. This was not turning out as he had expected. After all, God had taught him some of the handiest processes to make his life on the island easier to manage, but he had failed miserably at this one; that was for sure. He couldn't bear to think of how he would ever face God again after this crushing defeat let alone find a way to keep food around any longer, and that was critical to his survival.

Just as Alexander decided he might as well lie down and let death take him away, God reentered the picture and told him he needed only to forgive the seagulls for these horrible deeds and all would be well.

The young boy, who felt so angry and violated by these outrageous birds, did his best to put this all behind him and forgive the creatures who had in his mind obliterated his chances of ever eating again.

Night fell, and the boy went to bed hungry, tired, and filled with much apprehension about what the next day might possibly bring. He was so upset about everything that had happened thus far that he forgot to say his prayers.

During the night, God came to Alexander in a dream and asked him to consider a new way of finding forgiveness. He suggested the boy could think about the wrongs committed against him and allow himself to become lathered up about them again. While he was upset, he was to focus on where in his body he was feeling distress as he was doing this portion of the exercise. Upon realizing the location, for instance, in his solar plexus, he was to place his finger over the area, consider what he was angry about, and say aloud, "I am entitled to my feelings about this situation, and my feelings are free to move around in my body wherever they want." If the distress within moved to another place, he was to move his finger to that area. If that spot were unreachable, he would just focus on the placement point.

Next, he would give himself the opportunity to realize that whatever was ruffling his feathers so to speak was actually a mirror image of something in him that he had held against himself for some time. It may even be something he no longer did or thought but was something he did not like about himself in the past he had never forgiven himself for. As he realized that the birds were merely reflecting a mirror upon him, he realized also that that mirror was there to show him a shadow area in himself that he needed to forgive. That may seem the most unlikely thing at first thought, but if he focused on that, he would find that when he got into his brother's things without permission, he often broke or lost them, creating havoc for Devon to deal with.

This was much the same as what was happening to his food by these uninvited visitors.

Even within the dream, Alexander resisted this explanation. But upon further reflection, he admitted to himself that when he had broken his brother's precious belongings, he had felt really bad about that but had never known what to do about it besides apologize, which had never seemed enough.

The next part of this forgiveness puzzle would be for Alexander to ask God to show him the lesson here for all of them—the birds and his brother, who were in this drama with him though his brother was not physically there. God told him that the birds were looking to learn from him about sharing and love. They had entered an agreement before coming to this life that they would meet and have this skirmish so they could see that they were not the only ones on earth and would need to alter their behavior to accommodate the small boy if he asked them nicely to do so. The brother had entered a similar agreement.

"And so," God explained, "all parties involved are intertwined in a miraculous way. When you come into your lifetimes together, you depend on each other to show each other how to learn the lessons you came here to learn. When time passes and certain lessons are not learned in one scenario, you will encounter them in another and another until you are finally ready to release yourself and the others involved from the burden of carrying it.

"One release with the intensity brought forth by this method will clear the countless encounter lessons just like it that you have incurred. All you would need to do next would be to mentally thank those with whom you have shared this lesson and let them know you forgive them and love them completely as you do the same for yourself.

"Then, you would agree to release all concerned from the agreement you had with them as none of you will need it any longer. All these agreements, of course, would have taken place in heaven before any of you came into the lives you are leading.

"Last, allow yourself to drink in love from the universe as you bask in a vision of its light shining upon you."

The dream of wisdom imparting was complete. The youngster found himself drifting blissfully into a deep and restful sleep.

The next morning, Alexander awoke to a new day fully expecting another dose of the same chaos. But when he arose from his bed of leaves, he was pleased to discover he could not hear even a peep coming from the area where his food had been. He surveyed the remains and was surprised to see one seagull scratching where the food once sat. Too discouraged to shoo the gull away, the boy decided to let nature run its course. He tried to ignore the unwelcome guest.

That seemed to work but only for an instant. The seagulls returned in full force. *How could this be?* the young boy asked himself. *There's not even any food here to be attracting them!*

Alexander heard God say, "They need no food to attract them any longer. Your thoughts are doing that."

*This is just ridiculous!* the boy thought. *I can't attract things by just willing them! If that were the case, I would have willed those birds gone long ago!*

God replied, "You are attracting them by your thoughts of not wanting them. Whatever you intend to bring forth you will attract to yourself as long as you are not sending out opposing thoughts and therefore keeping them at bay.

"This seems more complicated than it really is, but if you want something, in that wanting, you have already asked the universe to provide it for you, and the universe instantly sets forth its powerful forces to bring that about. You have only to allow it to come into your experience. Do not resist it by putting your attention on its opposite. Like attracts like, and you must become a vibrational match with whatever it is you are wanting.

"When you think about what you don't want, it is drawn to you as if you were a magnet. You have full control over what you get and don't get. You have only to think about and talk about what you want instead of getting caught up in discussing and thinking about what you don't want. It's as simple as that!"

The one who called Himself God vanished and left the boy to deal with the mess once again on his own. But something had changed in him. And something seemed to have changed in the seagulls. It was almost as though they were there only for a last hurrah and to say goodbye. One by one, they began to leave, intending never again to invade the confines of his blessed island cave home.

# Chapter 7

## *Living in the Now*

Once upon a time in a far-off land, a young boy had come to know God in a delightful manner. In the past, he had considered himself alone in the world especially after his family had all but disappeared and he found himself stranded on this tropical island in the middle of nowhere.

At this point, whenever he had a problem, instead of turning to his mother, father, or older brother, he could turn only to God, who always had wise words and interesting lessons that would bring him eventually to a place of great understanding of the universe's miraculous ways.

One day, Alexander was thinking about every lesson he had learned, and that took him to a place in himself he never could have imagined he would be. There, he found what it meant to give himself completely over to whatever happened in his life on the island.

At times, he would wonder about what was happening back home, but those times were rare. His new way of living mindfully and paying strict attention to what he was doing each moment left little time for him to be missing those he had left behind.

One day, the mentor allowed him to visit his family in a dream, and he discovered there was still much love for him there. Those he had left behind were functioning quite well without him, but they still cared for him deeply.

He basked in the love he had felt from that delicious visit for the rest of the day. He had released himself to enjoy the experience no matter what it might bring his way.

# CHAPTER 8

# Meditation and Staying in Alignment with God Source Within

O nce upon a time, a boy named Alexander woke up all alone on an island in the middle of the Pacific. Every now and then, a cloud of sadness would descend on him and leave him feeling so alone that he would just huddle in his cave. Even the antics of his pet monkey could not lift his sense of gloom.

One such day, the one who lived on the faraway mountaintop and called Himself God appeared in the child's cave. He gently put his hand on the shoulder of the sobbing child and let him know there was always a way he could stay connected to everyone and everything he had known. He said there was a way of making himself a conduit of energy that would reach through the cosmos and touch those he had left behind including his parents and even his brother, Devon, with whom he had fought wildly at times.

God somehow knew that the night Alexander had fallen asleep and ended up on the desolate island, there had been a terrible fight between him and his big brother. His brother had been thoroughly upset with Alexander because of the mess he had caused with the older child's friends. Alexander had a way of getting so excited about things at times that he did not always watch what he said.

That time, he had fallen into that pattern again about his brother's book report of all things. He had seen it lying around and gave it a quick read out of curiosity. Surprisingly, he found it so intriguing that he spouted off about it to the neighborhood kids, and that completely embarrassed the learned writer. After all, Devon was a very private person. The information held there shined a light on the inner workings of his fascinating mind and exposed his confidential thoughts to potential adolescent ridicule. So much time had passed since then that Alexander was sure his brother would never forgive him.

God took him by the hand to a peaceful spot at the back of the cave and suggested Alexander get as comfortable as possible. If he preferred to lie on his back with his head on a pillow of grass, that was fine. He could also sit cross-legged.

Alexander opted to lie on his back and close his eyes. God guided him to an amazing level of relaxation by suggesting he would at first breathe slowly and deeply and watch each breath as he drew it in through his nose and blew it out through his mouth. With each breath, he would think that he was drawing in a breath of deep relaxation and breathing out all the stress and anxiety he felt. He was to imagine what he inhaled as a beautiful, loving elixir that comforted him completely and what he exhaled as containing sparks of nastiness carrying out any toxic feelings or anxiety he felt due to the fight with his brother or any other issue weighing on him. If he had no issues in mind at the time, he would just allow that thought to be a generic one.

After a few minutes of this relaxing process, God told Alexander a tale of the young boy going for a beautiful walk and seeing many unusual feats of nature including a magnificent beach much like the one outside the cave.

As Alexander was being guided, he noticed the beauty of nature in a new way. God described in such detail the unusual shapes and shadows of each plant and flower. They wandered from the beauty of the gently crashing waves to the thick of the jungle and then to a clearing where the boy found a splendid cot to lie on in the warm sun. The weather was sublime; there was just enough breeze, and the sky was such a deep blue that the trees leaned against it to rest their flickering leaves.

There was no other place the boy would rather have been than in that moment of peaceful repose. He felt so relaxed that he began to feel an energy flowing through his legs and extending up his body to his arms. It was an incredible experience, and he wanted to focus on what was happening in himself. Each time he felt his mind begin to wander, the energy would begin to fade, and he knew instinctively he had to redirect his attention to his breath and bask in this intensely peaceful experience.

He stayed there for quite some time before he realized God was no longer by his side. That unexpected realization shook him from his trance. As he slowly rose, he thought he would feel his aloneness once again. Instead, he felt as though the divine one had become a part of him in some way. He also felt a deep and residing sensation of serene rejuvenation.

# CHAPTER 9

## *Surrendering and Letting Go*

O nce upon a time, a small boy found himself alone on a beautiful island. He was accompanied only by a monkey companion named Manuka and a man who called Himself God. The God one called Himself that so the boy would not be confused about the fact that He actually was God Almighty. He set out to give the boy instructions that would lead him to that realization. Alexander had become so familiar with Him that he did not misunderstand the context in which this lesson unfolded.

One day when Alexander was frolicking with Manuka, God appeared again out of nowhere. The playing stopped immediately; the boy and the monkey knew by then that when the God one appeared, they had to pay close attention or risk missing a lesson that would catapult them to new dimensions of thought and realization.

The God one was at first a bit reserved that time in His demeanor, but He soon began to lay out a plan that if the boy followed would give him a very simple and easy way to live there on the island and in the world where his family was awaiting his return.

The plan was basic enough. Alexander had only to let go each time an idea, worry, or concern was plaguing him. He would find in the letting go that the God force in him would take over the situation.

At first, the boy did not know what God meant by letting go; that made no sense to him. But as God continued His eloquent explanation, Alexander realized if he just relaxed and released his attachment to the negative thought, he would find that the God force in him would swoop in and carry it for him in an amazing manner. That way of thinking about it alone would help him surrender whatever was happening in his life which was leading to strife.

As it began to sink in, God said that when Alexander was immersed in a surrender process, he should ask God to please take the reins, so to speak. The Universe would always be happy to oblige. That asking was highly important to God as well as to the person asking for the release of an issue. The Universe is elevated and expanded each time a blessing is bestowed, and the ones receiving the blessing are also enhanced.

Alexander soon discovered the truth of this when he tried the technique on the seagulls that had once again invaded his precious stock of foodstuffs. It took him so completely by surprise that at first, he forgot the lesson he had just learned at the hand of the Almighty. He was utterly incensed at the fact his cave was once again the place where nearly all the seagulls on the island had converged. He had already gone through the motions of appreciating their magnificent aspects, appreciating all that surrounded him, and thinking of them affectionately so they would feel the love that traveled through him to each of them even though they were making a mess of his cave again. Thankfully, they could not get into his food as he had taken care to keep only well sealed coconuts and bananas on hand since the last hard-learned lesson. But that did not keep them from throwing things about.

He wandered around outside the cave and wondered what he was missing there. Then he remembered the lesson he had learned that morning. It was so perfect he thought the hand of God must have been involved. How else would everything happening be so intertwined with his lessons in such perfect order?

After a bit of scrutinizing this epiphany, he went for a walk and decided to release his thoughts about this current drama into the universe and ask the God force within to take the reins and handle the details.

That was a new experience for this small boy who had never even believed there was a God let alone that he had a piece of God in himself. He realized that the piece of God he had within had the same mighty force God Almighty held.

These thoughts brought him back to a place of confusion, but instead of trying to figure it out, he decided to turn it over to his God force within and see what would come of it. Eventually, the one who called Himself God would return to give him the solace that his ways of thinking were right on—in a simplified manner that is.

The boy was informed that when he grew to a more mature level, all this would be explained to him further. But for the time being, God told him, "I will handle all your requests in the ways that best suit all concerned. Always."

# CHAPTER 10

# *God-Centered Thinking*

O nce upon a time, a boy named Alexander was nearly alone on a remote island. His companions were only a monkey named Manuka and a man who called Himself God.

One day, God told Alexander of a time when there was nothing at all except for God Almighty. There were no people or animals, no plants, land, or oceans. God decided He would like to have others to blend Himself with and teach each other lessons so He would expand by seeing how each person learned these lessons. He knew their perspectives would differ, and that would lend additional depth to whatever knowledge He had started with. Each of those involved would be a small part of God and give Him a front-row seat for all that would happen including the thoughts of each one involved and God's own thoughts as well.

To bring this about, God created heaven and earth and brought forth mountains and seas and everything in between. He set humanity on the earth along with all the magnificent animals that would support the ecosystem of this wondrous place. The way He brought this about is inconsequential to this story, but there are many theories that support the same end, so what does it really matter?

As soon as humanity began to increase, God allowed people to determine what they wanted to work on during each life they were allotted. Eventually, those who inhabited each time-space continuum would see the same characters over and over until they had such a connection with their soul friends from heaven that they would know each other on a certain level when they encountered each other in each lifetime they were working on.

That allowed God to provide an amazing attraction basis that ensured those who had made certain agreements from above would connect with each other on the earth plane in their given time-space allotments. Otherwise, they might live lives of complete chaos, and that was never the intention of the almighty, All That Is.

His intention was to bring together many who would interact in a mathematically enormous manner. No one would be able to keep track of the multitudes of strands of consciousness let alone the cross-overs of heavenly led situations that would wondrously occur, unless there actually was a higher power with infinite wisdom and strength. The amazing coincidences that would casually occur could never be pushed aside as mere accidents because they would often be astonishing. There would be no doubt in the minds of those involved that something larger than each of them had a hand in whatever heavenly imposed situation was taking place at any given time on earth.

There came a time, however, when the people began to believe that nothing was ever anything more than it appeared and that the powers of certain people would override the powers of God. There was no concrete evidence that there even was a God. The belief there was no God became somewhat commonplace as did the belief that people had created all the miracles after the initial big bang.

Once each species evolved into its current form, humans came to dominate the earth often with no regard for the sanctity of life except when it applied to each man's self and that of his own family and loved ones and sometimes their countries.

As the masses began to accept this secular outlook and consider it their fate, those who believed in God through their churches were often looked down upon. Their churches—pillars of strength in days gone by—were less effective in setting limits on people with respect to how they lived or their ultimate accountability to God.

Of course, many with a secular outlook demonstrated high levels of integrity, but the ways of many others became blurred because they did not check in with their inner God source when making decisions that would influence their honesty or sincerity.

In the days of God-centered thinking, people had only to check in with their inner God force to see whether their decisions would complement or be misaligned with others' decisions. That allowed for cut-and-dry, clear thinking on their parts and lessened their abilities to rationalize without crossing blatantly over the line of their higher selves' outlooks.

With the secular way of thinking increasingly prevalent across the planet, those who lean to that side—even if they believe in God in one way or another—have fallen to thought processes that lack accountability systems. They thus cross their own boundaries of morality much more easily.

This leads us to a point of needing to bring in Alexander once again, and so back to our story.

Once upon a time, a young boy was so overwhelmed by all this deep thought that he decided to take a break and swim in the ocean. He thought concertedly about all God had imparted to him. Alexander was realizing this God was indeed God Almighty. That realization alone was enough to bring him to his knees if it had not been for the fact that he was gliding through the water at the time.

He decided to give himself the space and time to put this into perspective. He would not make any determination about the validity of the information that had been revealed to him. It was of utmost importance to him that he maintained his relationship with the one who called Himself God. He thought that if he questioned anything the Holy One said, he would be forever banned from the endearing relationship they had established.

He wondered how he could ever tell anyone he was good friends with God Almighty and had heard these stories directly from the Source of all things. He had begun to question his beliefs and realize that the ways he had of making decisions and choices had more to do with what he wanted than with what God might think.

He decided that his interests and those of all concerned in anything he was mulling over would always be served best if he checked in with his inner God source, or higher self. That would make matters much easier and less complicated.

All this heavy thinking was making Alexander very hungry and tired, so he headed back to his cave, where he found Manuka and God immersed in a game of cards. They were having such a rip-roaring good time that he threw back his head in laughter and joined in the fun.

# CHAPTER 11

# Revisiting Intention Setting and Surrendering Control

O nce upon a time, a young boy named Alexander lived on a deserted island with only his monkey, Manuka, and his friend who called Himself God for company. He decided to give himself plenty of chances to practice his new tools and found many opportunities to do that on the island. His family remained in their beds at home, where he had left them when he escaped his old ways of thinking way back when.

One morning, he thought that he would soon go home but that while he was on the island, he had better dig deeper into some of the lessons the one called God had taught him. He had found that though they were quite beneficial, at times, he was not completely comfortable with the results brought about by some of the techniques he had been taught. He could easily remember to pave his way during times when he wanted to achieve something special, but normally, he would not remember to pave joyful and uplifting encounters for all concerned. Such times would often turn sour. If he only remembered to pave them as well, he would be in heaven on earth so to speak.

He realized he could ask God or the universe to direct the details of any endeavor; he had at last felt he was in a place of strong standing. That change in his procedure brought about remarkable differences in the ways he ultimately saw outcomes manifest. Alexander decided he would integrate this minor shift into his lesson plan.

# CHAPTER 12

# *Seeing God in Everyone and Everything*

O nce upon a time, a small boy who was at last ready to rejoin his family in their home on the shores of California had become quite accustomed to living in a cave on an island with only his friend Manuka, a monkey, and someone who called Himself God. God lived on a nearby mountaintop and came whenever he was summoned to offer astounding lessons in the most unusual ways.

The day he was preparing to leave, the boy became quite agitated about something that had occurred on the beach outside his cave. He focused on bringing his thought patterns back into alignment with his inner God source and was able to overcome his tendency to let his emotions fly out of control. That refreshingly freed him to continue tying up ends in order to return to his bed and pillow back home with the family he dearly missed.

One thing he needed to wrap up was how to keep in contact with the Divine after he was home. Another of course was how to maintain contact with Manuka, his beloved pet. With that in mind, Alexander and Manuka set out to look for God. They searched day and night for several days until God finally appeared out of nowhere in front of them. When they asked where He had been, He let them know in no uncertain terms that He had always been there. They needed only to open their eyes with the expectation of finding Him.

That was the final lesson for the boy before leaving the place he had called home for what seemed like years but had been only a speck of time in the scheme of things. That lesson would serve him like no other. No other lesson would give him the confidence that one would afford him. The formula alone would grant him everything he would need in life from then on without exception.

When the boy took that to heart, he decided to use this same process with Manuka. The monkey had become a part of him in many ways just as his realization of God had. As long as he held onto the love that had passed between them during his stay on the island, he would be able to open his eyes and behold the same love remaking itself back home only in other forms. This would be repeated, and he would soon become accustomed to seeing God in every other being he met just as he had realized Manuka had been another form of God all along.

Alexander had come a long way, but at the same time, he had gone nowhere. When he awoke the next morning, he was lying in his bed next to his brother's. The scent of bacon frying in the kitchen was all but overpowering in its call for him to jump out of bed and rejoin the family he so dearly loved and appreciated—almost more than his newborn appreciation for All That Is.

## CHAPTER 13

# The Ways of the World

O nce upon a time, a young boy named Alexander was awakened in the middle of the night by his dear friend Manuka, a monkey with very little thought to protocol. This monkey had crossed over the line of his imaginings and come into being in the realm of the youngster's home.

This created a bit of a problem for our dear Alexander as it had been so long since he had seen his little friend. He practically fell all over himself giving out all the love he could muster—and here it was the middle of the night with his brother sleeping in the next bed!

Alexander slipped out of bed, and the two twirled about in such a way that before they knew it they were back on the island where they had originally met. What a surprise that was for the youngster who had come to know it as his home way back when but had since made himself quite comfortable together again with his family in his California home.

There was much to do back on the island. None of Alexander's old stashes of food remained, and the cave he had called home during his last visit was inhabited by others who had made themselves quite at home. How strange it was to be seeing someone else in the cave that was so familiar to him yet no longer fit his ways of being.

In the days and months that had passed, many changes had taken place in his absence. The trees had grown, and the foliage was much more lush. The birds that had been so plentiful even to the extent of being problematic were swooping through the sky in the loveliest of formations. Not one was scavenging the beaches in search of food to be pilfered from unsuspecting sources.

The two young playmates set off to put things in order for themselves again. If this was where they would be staying for a while again, they wanted to fully embrace it. They loved one another so much and were practically ecstatic at the thought of blending their talents in new ways. It had been such a long time since they had had each other to interact with, though something quite different had taken place on the level of their consciousness that notices such things.

Never before had either experienced the closeness they felt. In the past, their friendship had been close and had frolicked along merrily, but now, they felt more deeply connected in some way. They had a sense that they could even read each other's thoughts. That turn of events interested them. The boy was in search of connections like no other, and the monkey was open to seeing what might develop as they lived again on this magnificent island where they had developed such a deep and abiding friendship long ago.

One morning in the new way of seeing things, Alexander awoke to find Manuka sleeping lazily over in the corner of the new cave he called home for the time being. The little guy had fallen asleep in such an endearing manner that our young friend could not bear to awaken him.

Watching him fondly, Alexander realized the similarities between the monkey and everyone he had ever met. The expression on his face matched his mother's sweet smile, his father's arched eyebrow, his brother's dimpled cheek, and so on. He thought about all the people he knew and how they all seemed to appear in one way or another on the face of his beloved Manuka.

Never before had he seen so many similarities to others he knew on the face of another. There had been times when someone had reminded him of his dad or brother, but never all his family members, friends, and acquaintances. The experience was mind-blowing to him. He had not recognized that this had been the case all along with everyone he had met or known. Each person had a connection to each other through their God force, and Manuka was symbolizing that for him right before his eyes. *Why haven't I seen that before? Now it's so clear that it's as if I had always known it.*

The question was what to do with this bit of knowing that had taken him by storm in the middle of the night in his bed back home. After much consideration, Alexander decided he would proceed with his life on the shores of his family home in California and forevermore give himself opportunities to expand his learning of this amazing phenomenon so he would become so intertwined with his God self that he would no longer know the difference between his selves in this way.

The God force within can be so encompassing if we allow this that we can no longer tell the difference between ourselves and the Godhead. When we come to that point in our expansion, we are ready to break out of the mold of needing to control everything that comes before us. When we finally decide to release that control and give it to God to handle, we will find ourselves in a place bordering on heaven.

And in heaven lies the answers to all things and All That Is.

# CHAPTER 14

## *Beginning to See Within*

O nce upon a time, a boy named Alexander awoke one morning to find he had had an amazing dream. His dream had encompassed many subjects including the return to the island he had spent so much time on during his previous way of thinking while he was preparing for this major change taking place in him.

One of the subjects regarded his monkey friend, Manuka, who had revealed himself to be the actual Godhead within and whom Alexander would relate to in a new way forever after having had this dream in which he realized the enormity of what he had experienced.

From here on out, he would strive to be connected to Manuka at all costs. Even the disdainful thoughts of others would not dissuade him from his newfound connection and how important it would be for him to realize always even when he was wondering about the integration of such knowledge.

He would also take every opportunity to see the God self in everyone and everything including the ways the universe handed him lessons at the cost of his feathers getting ruffled at times. Instead of ruffling back, he decided he would step back and allow his center to unfold once again before stepping forward and responding. That would entail his silence at times, which would be a new undertaking for him. In the past, his responses would at times jump out before he could stop himself. Now that he realized with his entire being that he was always connected to his divine or higher self, he would remember to be more deliberate in his responses.

When others would utter changes in plans that would take him by surprise, he would be much better equipped to reply as he had given himself space to find the all-important connection before jumping out with a response. That would be a treasure beyond treasures and bring forth astounding payoffs to his life. And forevermore, he would be finding in himself a new way of looking at life—through the lens of his God self.

# BIBLIOGRAPHY

Abraham, Esther and Jerry Hicks. *The Amazing Power of Deliberate Intent.* Carlsbad, CA: Hay House, 2006.

Dyer, Dr. Wayne. *The Power of Intention.* Carlsbad, CA: Hay House, 2004.

Myss, Caroline. *Sacred Contracts: Awakening Your Divine Potential.* New York: Three Rivers, 2002.

Singer, Michael. *the untethered soul: the journey beyond yourself.* Oakland, CA: New Harbinger Publications and Noetic Books, 2007.

Tipping, Colin. *Radical Forgiveness.* Boulder, CO: Sounds True, 2009.

## About the Author

LouAnne Ludwig has firsthand experience using metaphysical practices to give her everything she desires and more. She brings this same experience to others in a simple way that demonstrates how easy it is to change our lives for the better and infuse them with new meaning and balance.

Her empathic practice in dream analyzing has assisted hundreds to cut through their defenses helping them to see exactly what they need to bring peace and harmony into their everyday lives.

She lives in Southern California.

Visit her at www.louanneludwig.com

CPSIA information can be obtained
at www.ICGtesting.com
Printed in the USA
BVHW031957080219
539844BV00001B/12/P